PIG

plays Cupid

Barbara Catchpole

Illustrated by metaphrog

Ransom

Love

This story is about love.

Elephants fall in love.

Mice fall in love.

Even teachers fall in love. I know, I was stuck in a stockroom with two of them. It made me a little bit sick in my mouth.

I suppose that's where other teachers come from - teachers falling in love. Yeuchh!

I was in love with Tiffany Brigstock in my class.

It must be one of the great love stories of our time: Posh and Becks, Will and Kate, Pig and Tiff.

It came to a tragic end when I farted in assembly. My mum said

'Your dad farted all the time. Wherever he is, I bet he's farting right now!'

and

    'All blokes do it.'

and

    'That's how they sell so much air freshener.
    It's not because of smelly DOGS.'

Anyway, Tiffany won't talk to me now, even
though my tummy is back to normal.

Also the ginger dinner lady still secretly gives
me baked beans at lunch, even though the
headteacher said she wasn't to do it.

All my family have problems with love.

Suki

Suki is still going out with Lee the milkman. It's been hard on all of us.

There's all the tears when they break up.

Then there's all the tears when they get back together.

There's tears when they watch television.

There's tears when they
stop watching television
and have a row.

There's tears when they
make up.

I just wish Lee would stop crying. Suki thinks it's
funny.

Gran

Gran's husband, Bill, was a good bloke. I can remember him — just. He used to give me sweets. He did jigsaws with me when I was little.

I'm still little, but Mum says I'll have a growth spurt soon:

'Probably coming up to Christmas, when nobody's got any money to buy you clothes.

'I think you do it so that nobody will have money for presents. Just try to stop your feet growing. I can't afford trainers.'

Gran keeps Bill's ashes in a big thermos flask thing on the coffee table.

She put sticky tack under it to fix it on the table. She sellotaped the top on because I kept

Knocking into it and she

'Doesn't want to have to hoover Bill up or get bits of fluff in him.'

(I'm sure he wouldn't mind.)

Gran talks to him all the time.

'Shall we have a cup of tea, Bill?'

'It's Pig, Bill, isn't that nice?'

'Time for bed, Bill.'

Of course, he doesn't say anything back, but at night time she even takes him upstairs and puts him on the little table next to the bed.

Mum says

'It makes her feel better. And, of course, she's mad as cheese.'

Harry

Mum says hamsters don't really like other hamsters. They fight all the time.

They only get together to make babies.

She said:

> 'At least Mrs Hamster doesn't have to
> worry about Mr Hamster bogging off to
> Spain without so much as a kiss goodbye.'

My mum

The other day I got a postcard from my dad.
It had a picture of a donkey with a straw hat
on the front.

He had written on
the back. (I mean my
dad wrote on the back

14

of the postcard. The donkey didn't write on the back of the postcard. Or on my dad's back.)

(Just to be clear, my dad didn't write it on the back of the donkey, either. That never works because you can't get donkeys through letterboxes.)

Dad had written:

'OK Pig? Hola from Spain!

Having a great time.

Got a job and everything.

Come out and see me!

Love from your old dad.

XXXXXX'

I put it on the fridge with a magnet.

'Can I go to Spain?'

I asked Mum.

'Oh yes – I'll just pack your bag. I'll get

your air fare out of the Post Office. You

can pop over for the weekend! Go find your flip flops!'

Now, I may not be the brightest light on the Christmas tree, but I knew Mum was joking about that. Since Dad left, she's been a bit sad and a bit angry.

She used to have her hair a lovely white-blonde colour. The stuff stank the house out. She's stopped doing it. She's stopped putting on her red lipstick, too. She looks older.

I don't care that he's gone. I'm fine. Doesn't bother me. I just happened to slam the door a bit on my way out of the kitchen. The wind blew it, that's all.

I went back in to say 'sorry' and Mum was sitting there. She was holding the postcard. She was turning it over and over.

I think she was crying.

It was all Raj's fault

I told Raj what had happened because, with all his sisters, he understands about girls. He's got seven sisters.

Raj understands most things, but not everything. He doesn't understand how to get into the bathroom before they do, or how to get them out once they are in there (or how to get them to pick up the underwear and towels they leave on the floor).

Raj has been known to walk round to our house to go to the toilet.

Raj said:

'I know just how we can help your mum.
On my computer there is a website. You
can put your name in and it will find you a
man to go out with. It says 'for fun and
friendship'!'

I said:

'But I don't want a man to go out with!'

'Not YOUR name, you dipstick! Your mum's
name. We can use one of my sister's email
addresses to pick up the messages and fix
your mum up with a new man.

'I know Tav's password. If we find your

mum a rich man, you'll probably get bought loads of stuff and get taken on holiday.'

Perhaps he would take me to Spain.

The website

So we logged onto the 'Kissy Kissy Fun and Friendship' website.

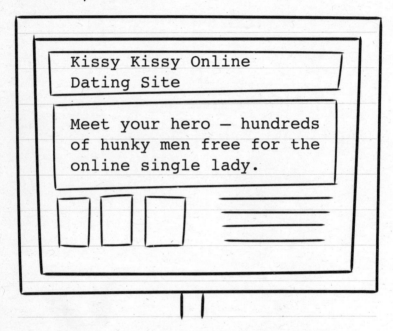

Raj's parents trust him to behave with the computer. This is because all his sisters can be trusted. His parents really don't know anything at all about bringing up boys.

This is what I wrote about my mum:

'I am thirty years old.'

(She might be about forty now. I
don't really know. Forty-five?)

'I have beautiful blonde hair.'

(She could have, anyway, if she just
did it from the packet again.)

'I like ballet, the opera and eating in posh
restaurants.'

(She likes Eastenders, bingo and chips.)

'I have a wonderful, clever son.'

(She has a wonderful, clever son.)

'I want to meet a man of a similar age with no children for chat and going out.'

(I said 'with no children' because, if they get on, the bloke can spend all his money on me. New football boots first, I think. My boots seem to have got too small for my feet. And the colour's getting old.)

Do you watch 'House' on telly? He's this really scruffy old doctor who is rude to everyone. My Mum says he's lovely.

I like it because his patients explode with blood or sick or pus at least once an episode, sometimes three or four times.

They never die because he's so clever and rude to people. He drills into their brains or chops a bit off them or something.

Anyway, Raj said the same thing that House says all the time:

'Everybody lies.'

To tell you the truth, I think all grown-ups do lie a bit. And that's not a lie.

The photo

We had to upload a photo, so I tried to take one of Mum with my phone. I just got lots of photos of her holding her hand in front of her

face and shouting

'Nooooooooooo! Pig!'

at me.

So we used an old one from about ten years
ago. Raj scanned it in. Raj is like Bill Gates but
smaller – and Sikh.

Nothing like Bill Gates, then – but still a genius
with computers.

27

The new men

Raj said we should choose two blokes, not one.

He said whenever he asked a girl out, he asked two because one would not turn up. He said, quite a lot of the time, neither girl turned up.

I like Raj, he's my friend, but I can see why that might happen. Perhaps he will be a girl magnet after he has grown his beard. It will hide his face.

Raj says it will happen any day now.

All the people on the website used made-up names, to keep their real names a secret.

We called Mum 'Blondie'. Raj wanted to call her 'Hotlips' but I got angry because, after all, SHE'S MY MUM. So he backed down. There will be no 'Kissy Kissy' stuff in our house. Just the fun and friendship.

The two men we chose were called 'Lonely Guy' and 'Millionaire'. I was rooting for Millionaire!

This is what they said about themselves:

Hi Blondie!

I am almost thirty five and I am very good looking. I am nearly six foot tall and very athletic. I enjoy skiing, hang gliding and jazz. I love children but I couldn't eat a whole one (LOL). I want to meet someone to share my jet-set lifestyle.

Hi Lonely Guy!

(OK so far!)

I am a beautiful single mum.

    (Well, she looks a bit ratty at the

    moment, but she could pull herself

    together and sort herself out.)

I enjoy all sports.

    (She enjoys all sweets and rides a

    motorbike.)

My son is very clever and an ace

footballer.

    (True. I've even been moved up a

    Maths set because Tiffany's parents

    said I was a Bad Influence. And

    I'm sure I will be in the first

    football team when I tell my lovey

dovey, Kissy wissy PE teacher what I heard him saying to the art teacher in the English stockroom.)

Looking forward to meeting you!

Blondie

I am pleased to meet you, Blondie. I am a single man who is a very young sixty. I too like opera. Which is the best one, do you think? I also like jazz and Sudoku puzzles. I have no family and I would love to meet yours.

Raj said all grown-ups say they like jazz because they think it makes them look cool. He says jazz is music that goes for a walk and keeps tripping up all the time. It makes his head hurt.

I don't know about jazz, but it was true: everybody on the site was 'into jazz'. Also everybody was rich, which was good, because we aren't.

From Tkaur@mailmail.com

To: Millionaire@supanet.com

Hi Millionaire!

(OK so far!)

I am a beautiful single mum.

nice

(She's nice inside. I
don't mean all the
blood and bits and pus
you see inside on
'House'. My mum is a
nice person. She's also
very scary, so I've got
to get this right.)

My favourite opera is 'The Magic Flute'.
(Raj printed a big list off the
computer, closed his eyes and stuck
a pin in it. When his finger had
stopped bleeding, we decided there
was the most blood on 'The Magic
Flute'.)

My family is a quiet and loving family. We go to the opera a lot together.

(EVERYBODY LIES.)

Our lovely home

Raj and I asked Millionaire and Lonely Guy to come to our lovely home at seven o'clock on Saturday, so that they could pick Mum up to go hang gliding or watch opera or some other grown-up rubbish.

I asked Raj what I should do if they both turned up. He said that never happened.

He said if I was worried, I could tell Mum

36

what we had done before they came.

I thought about telling Mum. I think that was
when I started to be really worried.

I really wanted to fart, but I tried not to. We
were in Raj's bedroom and I thought it would
be a bit rude.

For a while nothing happened. At last, I thought, I can control my super power!

But, no, it still happened and it was worse for holding it in.

Raj sniffed and said:

> 'You ARE worried aren't you, Pig? It will be fine, I promise you. Open the window, will you? Quickly, Pig! The window! I'm choking!'

I live in a council house next to a chip shop. We sent the two blokes the right address, but the picture we sent them to help them find it was a picture of Buckingham Palace.

Saturday night

By seven o'clock I was terrified. Why, oh, why had I done this? I must be mad!

Mum was really going to go off on one about this! She was upstairs in the bathroom.

Suki was having a night in. She only does it to wind Lee up and make him cry.

Gran was cleaning out the hamster. Harry was in his high-security prison: the bread bin with a brick on top.

By half-past seven I felt better. By eight o'clock I was OK. They weren't going to come! Thank you, thank you, thank you!

Then there was loud and angry knocking on our front door.

THUMP! THUMP! THUMP!

Mum stomped down the stairs in her ratty old dressing gown with a towel wrapped round her head.

She opened the door and two strange (very, VERY strange) men stood there.

One was a teenager (he looked like Justin Bieber, stupid hair and stupid grin). He was also very, very short and small. I didn't see him at all until Mum turned round.

The other one was a really old man. He had a

huge white beard. He looked just like Santa Claus

out of uniform.

They both held a big bunch of red roses. That is, they held a bunch each. They weren't sharing the same one. My English teacher says I have to make things clear. That's why I was going on about the postcard and the donkey.

I looked at them: Santa Claus and a tiny Justin Bieber.

Then I remembered:

EVERYBODY LIES.

Run!

They both said at the same time:

'I'm from Kissy Kissy Dating Agency. Have I come to the right house?'

My mum turned round and shouted:

'P-I-I-I-I-G !'

– at the same time that I ran out of the back door.

A happy ending for everyone except Lee

I hid behind the front garden wall. Mum was going to murder me!

Justin and Santa had both gone into the house. The light was on in the room at the front (the room we hardly ever use).

I was cold and I knew Mum was going to be livid. She wanted George Clooney, not those two love rejects.

Then an amazing thing happened. The front door opened and Justin came out with Suki. He only came up to her shoulder. Gran came out with Santa. What was going on?

Mum shouted from the hall:

'Pig! Get your bum in here!'

She actually sounded OK, so I took a chance.

She only shouted at me for thirty minutes, which is not a record, believe me. Her record is fifty-two minutes. I timed it on the clock on the shelf in the Room We Don't Use Much.

I don't really listen when she shouts like this, but it did go on a bit:

'... One of the most stupid ... that Raj wants his head examining ... mind your own business ... plain dangerous ... grounded for a month ... phoning Mrs Kaur ... how dare you ... could have been axe murderers ... or terrorists ... your dad's got a lot to answer for ... sitting on his bum on a beach in Spain ... leaving me struggling with his bonkers son ... can look after myself, which is more than you can ... no pocket money ... phone social services ... sell you on eBay ... can live under the stairs like Harry Potter ... what on earth were you thinking ... grade 'A' plonker ... don't know why I ever had kids ... '

There was a lot more I can't remember. In the end she had to stop because she ran out of breath and felt dizzy.

It turned out that Justin went clubbing with Suki and she really liked him:

'He's got a few bob and he's a laugh.'

She's going to dump Lee, but she hasn't told him yet. Bet he cries. Mum says we'll miss the milk.

Gran went to Bingo with Santa and they're going next week as well. It's a rollover.

Gran's put Bill in a cupboard in the kitchen, in case Santa and Bill see each other. She thinks Bill might get a bit upset.

My mum said:

'Mad as two balloons!'

Harry escaped from the bread bin during all the fuss. How does he do that? It had a brick on it!

We haven't captured him yet. We see him every now and again strolling across the kitchen floor. Mum says he raises a paw and waves at us.

I reckon he's making a rude sign.

49

Mum again

When Mum had finished shouting, she needed chips and a bit of a sit down, so I went next door to buy some food.

I had to do it with the pocket money she had taken back from me, because I-am-never-having-pocket-money-ever-again.

When I got back, the postcard was gone from the fridge. I didn't say anything about it. It didn't matter.

As I got the chips onto the plates, she stood up in front of the mirror.

'You know what, though, Pig. You were right.

Time to move on.'

She took the towel off her hair and it fell down,

long, lovely and white blonde.

Suddenly I felt happy and sad at the same

time.

The next **PIG** book is

PIG
gets the
Black Death
(nearly)

About the author

Barbara Catchpole was a teacher for thirty years and enjoyed every minute. She has three sons of her own who were always perfectly behaved and never gave her a second of worry.

Barbara also tells lies.